HEATHER HAS TWO MOMMIES

WRITTEN BY

LESLÉA NEWMAN

ILLUSTRATED BY

DIANA SOUZA

ALYSON
WONDERLAND

Also by Lesléa Newman:

JUST LOOKING FOR MY SHOES
GOOD ENOUGH TO EAT
LOVE ME LIKE YOU MEAN IT
A LETTER TO HARVEY MILK
BUBBE MEISEHS BY SHAYNEH MAIDELEHS
(edited by Lesléa Newman)

Bookcovers by Diana Souza:

WILDFIRE: IGNITING THE SHE/VOLUTION
by Sonia Johnson
ZAMI: A BIOMYTHOGRAPHY
by Audre Lorde
POEMS
by Rita Mae Brown
THE INNER DANCE
by Diane Mariechild
THE PROSPERINE PAPERS
by Jan Clausen

This is an Alyson Wonderland title from Alyson Publications,
40 Plympton St., Boston, Mass. 02118.
Distributed in the U.K. by GMP Publishers, P.O. Box 247, London, N17 9QR, England.
Library of Congress Catalog Card Number: 89-85230
ISBN 1-55583-180-X
5 4 3

HEATHER HAS TWO MOMMIES
for Sarah and Miranda Crane and all of their friends

Many thanks to:

The hundreds of people whose contributions helped publish this book; to Nancy Braus for her generous support; to Aro Veno for bringing us all together; to Dana Lee Kingsbury, the five-year-old artist who drew the children's pictures in this book; and to Clover for asking Lesléa to write a book for her daughter Sarah.

This is Heather. She lives in a little house with a big apple tree in the front yard and lots of tall grass in the back yard.

Heather's favorite number is two. She has two arms, two legs, two eyes, two ears, two hands and two feet. Heather has two pets: a ginger colored cat named Gingersnap and a big black dog named Midnight.

Heather also has two mommies: Mama Jane and Mama Kate.

A long long time ago, before Heather was born, Mama Jane and Mama Kate were very good friends. Only they weren't mommies then. They were just Jane and Kate. Kate lived on one side of town with Midnight and Jane lived on the other side of town with Gingersnap.

After they were friends for a long long time, Kate and Jane realized that they were very much in love with each other. They decided they wanted to live together and be a family together. So Jane and Kate and Midnight and Gingersnap all moved into the little house with the big apple tree in the front yard and the tall grass in the back yard and they were all very happy except for one thing.

Kate and Jane wanted to have a baby. After they talked about it for a long time they decided the baby would grow in Jane's womb. A womb is a special place inside a woman where babies grow. Jane ate lots of good food and got plenty of rest so she would be strong and healthy to carry the baby.

Kate and Jane went to see a special doctor together. After the doctor examined Jane to make sure that she was healthy, she put some sperm into Jane's vagina. The sperm swam up into Jane's womb. If there was an egg waiting there, the sperm and the egg would meet, and the baby would start to grow.

Jane and Kate waited and waited to see if the sperm and the egg had started to grow into a baby. About a month went by. Then Jane said she felt a little funny. She was hungry a lot and her breasts felt tender. After another month went by, Jane's belly started getting bigger. There was a baby growing inside of Jane's womb! Kate and Jane were so happy! They hugged each other and kissed each other and laughed so hard that they cried.

This is what Jane looked like right before Heather was born. Her belly grew so big she had to get all new clothes. Kate put her hands on Jane's belly to feel the baby kick. "She's strong," Kate said.

Soon it was time for Heather to be born. Jane sat up in bed and pushed and pushed. A special nurse called a mid-wife was there to help. Kate was there to help too. When the baby's head was showing, the mid-wife stepped back and out popped baby Heather, right into Kate's arms.

Heather was a very tiny baby with big brown eyes and lots of brown curly hair. When she was very little mostly she ate a lot and slept a lot. Sometimes she smiled and sometimes she cried.

Now Heather is three years old. Her mommies take turns taking care of her. She likes to do different things with each of her mommies. Mama Kate is a doctor. Heather likes to listen to her heartbeat with a real stethoscope. When Mama Kate has a headache, Heather gives her two aspirins. When Heather has a cut on her knee, she asks Mama Kate to put two band-aids on it.

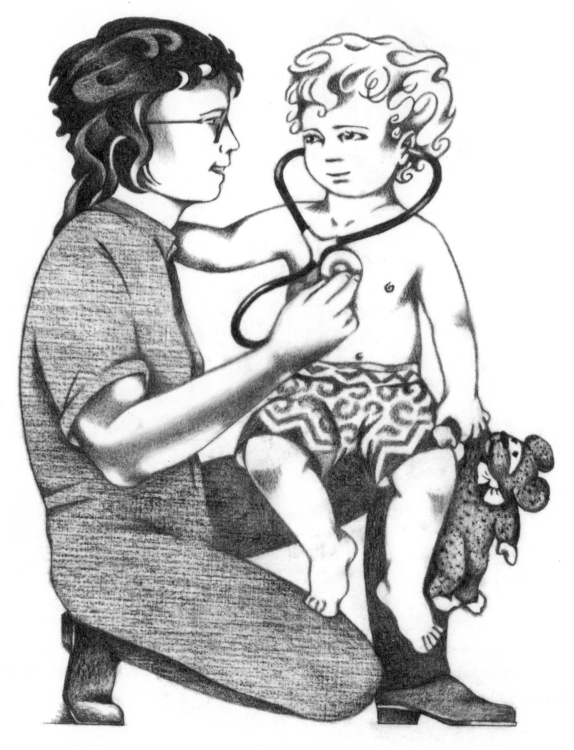

Mama Jane is a carpenter. Heather likes to look in her toolbox. She has nails and screws and a long yellow tape measure. Mama Jane has two hammers: a big one for herself and a little one for Heather. Mama Jane and Heather are building a table together.

On weekends Heather and her two mommies are all together. They do lots of fun things. On sunny days they go to the park. On rainy days they stay inside and bake cookies. Heather likes to eat two gingersnaps and drink a big glass of milk.

One day Mama Kate and Mama Jane tell Heather they have a surprise for her. ''You're going to be in a play group,'' Mama Kate says. ''With lots of other kids and a teacher named Molly,'' Mama Jane says. Heather feels a little excited and a little scared. "Can Midnight and Gingersnap come too?'' she asks. ''No, they have to stay home,'' Mama Jane says. ''But you can bring two special things with you,'' Mama Kate says. Heather picks out her favorite blue blanket to sleep with at nap time and her favorite red cup to drink out of at lunch time. Now she feels a little less scared.

The next day Mama Kate and Mama Jane bring Heather to Molly's house.

Molly has lots of fun things to play with: books and puzzles, crayons and paint, building blocks and dress up clothes. There's a big round table where Heather can eat her lunch and a quiet corner where Heather can take her nap. While Mama Jane and Mama Kate talk to Molly, Heather puts two puzzles together all by herself.

Soon the other children come and it's time for Mama Jane and Mama Kate to leave. They kiss Heather goodbye and Heather cries. But only a little.

It's lots of fun being at Molly's house. Heather builds a big tower out of building blocks and gets all dressed up like a firefighter. She paints two pictures at the easel--one for Mama Jane and one for Mama Kate. She drinks apple juice out of her favorite red cup at lunch time and she sleeps in the quiet corner with her favorite blue blanket at nap time.

After nap time, everyone sits in a circle and Molly reads them a story. The story is about a little boy whose father is a veterinarian. He takes care of dogs and cats and birds and fish and hamsters when they get sick. "My daddy's a doctor too," Juan says, pointing at the book. "He takes care of sick people." "My daddy's a teacher," David says. "Once I went to his school with him."

"I don't have a daddy," Heather says. She'd never thought about it before. Did everyone except Heather have a daddy? Heather feels sad and begins to cry.

Molly picks up Heather and gives her a hug. "Not everyone has a daddy," Molly says. "You have two mommies. That's pretty special. Miriam doesn't have a daddy either. She has a mommy and a baby sister. That's pretty special too."

"I don't have any mommies. I have two daddies," Stacy says proudly. "I have two daddies too," Joshua says. "My mommy and my step-daddy live in a blue house and my daddy lives by himself in a yellow house."

"Let's all draw pictures of our families," Molly says. The children all sit at the big round table and Molly hands out paper and crayons.

This is Juan's picture. Juan has a mommy and a daddy and a big brother named Carlos.

This is Miriam's picture. Miriam's mommy is pushing her baby sister on a swing in the park. Miriam is big enough to swing on the swings all by herself.

This is Stacy's picture. Stacy's daddies are both tall. Stacy likes to sit in between them on the big red couch in their living room and listen to a story.

This is Joshua's picture. Joshua's mommy and step-father are dropping him off at his daddy's house. Some days Joshua stays with his mommy and his step-father, and some days he stays with his daddy.

This is David's picture. David has a mommy and a daddy and two brothers and a sister. No one in David's family looks alike because all of the children are adopted. One of David's brothers uses a wheelchair.

When the children are finished, Molly hangs up all the pictures and everyone looks at them. "It doesn't matter how many mommies or how many daddies your family has," Molly says to the children. "It doesn't matter if your family has sisters or brothers or cousins or grandmothers or grandfathers or uncles or aunts. Each family is special. The most important thing about a family is that all the people in it love each other."

Soon Heather's mommies come to take her home. Gingersnap and Midnight come too. First Heather shows them all the pictures. "Is that me?" Mama Kate asks pointing at Heather's picture. "And is that me?" Mama Jane asks, pointing too.

Heather looks at her picture. "This is the mommy I love the best," she says, pointing to the mommy who has big round glasses just like Mama Kate. "And this is the mommy I love the best," Heather says pointing to the mommy who has short red hair just like Mama Jane.

Mama Kate and Mama Jane both laugh and give Heather a great big hug. Heather gives each of her mommies two kisses. Mama Jane takes Heather's right hand and Mama Kate takes Heather's left hand and then Heather and Mama Kate and Mama Jane and Midnight and Gingersnap all go home.

ABOUT THE AUTHOR:

Lesléa Newman

has one mommy, one daddy, one grandma and two brothers. She has been writing stories and poems ever since she was a little girl. Lesléa now lives in Northampton, Massachusetts with a woman she loves named Mary, and their two cats, Couscous and Poony Cat. She is a teacher as well as a writer. This is her first children's book.

Photo: SUE TYLER

ABOUT THE ILLUSTRATOR:

Diana Souza

Illustrates and designs for authors and publishers throughout the nation from her enchanted temple studio in Ithaca, New York.

Photo: KAT DALTON

Other ALYSON WONDERLAND titles

(Books for younger children are described first here.)

DADDY'S ROOMMATE, by Michael Willhoite, $9.00. This is the first book written for the children of gay men. The large, full-color illustrations depict a boy, his father, and the father's lover as they take part in activities familiar to all kinds of families: cleaning the house, shopping, playing games, fighting, and making up. Winner of a Lambda Literary Award. Ages 2 to 6.

• "This picture book is an auspicious beginning to the Alyson Wonderland imprint. Willhoite's text is suitably straightforward, and the format is easily accessible to the intended audience. The colorful characters with their contemporary wardrobes and familiar surroundings lend the tale a stabilizing air of warmth and familiarity." — *Publishers Weekly*

FAMILIES, by Michael Willhoite, $3.00. Many kinds of families, including a diversity of races, generations, and cultural backgrounds, are depicted in this coloring book (which is accompanied by a short text); several of the families include lesbian or gay parents. Ages 3 to 6.

• "*Families* contains excellent line drawings by award-winning *Washington Blade* artist Michael Willhoite. Willhoite's illustrations, along with the minimal text, convey the many varieties of families that exist today in words and images children can easily grasp." — *Wisconsin Light*

THE DADDY MACHINE, by Johnny Valentine, with illustrations by Lynette Schmidt, $7.00. In a fantasy reminiscent of Dr. Seuss, two kids with lesbian mothers fantasize about what it would be like to have a father. When their mothers go away for the day, the kids make themselves a daddy machine, and soon they get their wish: They turn on the machine, and a dad pops out. Then comes another, and another, and another. "Sue," the narrator says, "we did a good job, but we're kind of in a fix. The machine is great, but we missed one thing. It doesn't have an OFF switch!" Ages 4 to 8.

• *"The Daddy Machine* is a wonderfully illustrated story of a lesbian family complete with dog, cat and parakeet. The book made me laugh out loud, and that is not easy in this serious world." — *Sappho's Isle*

GLORIA GOES TO GAY PRIDE, by Lesléa Newman; illustrated by Russell Crocker, $8.00. Gay Pride Day is fun for Gloria, and for her two mothers. Here, the author of *Heather Has Two Mommies* describes, from the viewpoint of a young girl, just what makes up this special day. Ages 4 to 7.

• "Leslea Newman has continued the pioneering work she began in 1989 with *Heather Has Two Mommies*. This book rings very true. Russell Crocker's illustrations are simple yet eloquent pencil drawings which contain much sensitivity and scope." — *Off Our Backs*

THE ENTERTAINER, by Michael Willhoite, $4.00. The award-winning author and illustrator of *Daddy's Roommate* takes a new approach here: a story told entirely in pictures. Fame and fortune come to Alex, a talented boy who loves to juggle — until he discovers what's really important in life. Ages 3 to 8.

• "In a series of charming illustrations reminiscent of Maurice Sendak, Willhoite takes us on a journey with Alex, the young hero. This is a tender and beautifully *told* story which proves that Willhoite's elegantly realized pictures are, indeed, worth thousands of words." — *Lambda Book Report*

BELINDA'S BOUQUET, by Lesléa Newman; illustrated by Michael Willhoite, $7.00. Upon hearing a cruel comment about her weight, young Belinda decides she wants to go on a diet. But then her friend Daniel's lesbian mom tells her, "Your body belongs to you," and that just as every flower has its own special kind of beauty, so does every person. Belinda quickly realizes she's fine just the way she is. Ages 4 to 8.

• "The family situation and characters are inviting possibilites. Cartoon illustrations by Willhoite are amiably and disarmingly suburban." — *The Bulletin of the Center for Children's Books*

written by **Lesléa Newman**
illustrated by **Michael Willhoite**

A BOY'S BEST FRIEND, by Joan Alden; illustrated with photos by Catherine Hopkins, cloth, $13.00. Will, a seven-year-old asthma sufferer, has proclaimed that he wants nothing at all for his birthday if he can't have a dog. He sees his birthday come and almost go without a gift. But at the last hour, Will's two moms present him with a dog who will make a difference by being different. Ages 4 to 8.

A BOY'S BEST FRIEND

By Joan Alden
Illustrated by Catherine Hopkins

THE DUKE WHO OUTLAWED JELLY BEANS AND OTHER STORIES, by Johnny Valentine, illustrated by Lynette Schmidt, cloth, $13.00. After he outlawed jelly beans, the duke issued another proclamation: "I had exactly one mother and one father, and I turned out so well, I think *all* children should have exactly one mother and one father. Any that don't ... why, we'll throw 'em in the dungeon." But the kids of the kingdom found a way to stop him. Their story is one of five original and enchanting fairy tales that make up this collection. Beautifully illustrated with paintings and drawings throughout. Winner of a Lambda Literary Award. Ages 5 to 10.

• "One of the outstanding children's books of the season." — *Robert Hale, in The Horn Book Magazine*

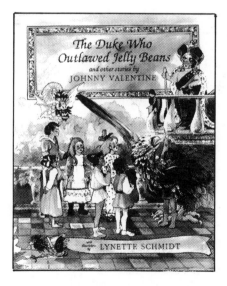

The Duke Who Outlawed Jelly Beans
and other stories by
JOHNNY VALENTINE

LYNETTE SCHMIDT

THE DAY THEY PUT A TAX ON RAINBOWS, by Johnny Valentine; illustrated by Lynette Schmidt, cloth, $13.00. Three brothers use their unique talents to discover hidden treasure ... a girl is washed off her boat during a storm and discovers a kingdom beneath the sea ... and a young boy saves his village from a future without rainbows. These three new fairy tales, by the author and illustrator of *The Duke Who Outlawed Jelly Beans,* feature the adventures of kids who happen to have lesbian and gay parents. Ages 5 to 10.

THE GENEROUS JEFFERSON BARTLEBY JONES, by Forman Brown; illustrated by Leslie Trawin, $8.00. Jefferson Bartleby Jones is lucky to have two dads, because one is always free to have fun with him on the weekends. He generously loans out one dad to a friend, then the other — and suddenly discovers himself home all alone for the first time. Forman Brown's lively verse gives kids with two dads a lot to feel good about. Ages 5 to 8.
• "A delightful, whimsical story of a boy with two dads."
— *This Week in Texas*

HOW WOULD YOU FEEL IF YOUR DAD WAS GAY?, by Ann Heron and Meredith Maran; illustrated by Kris Kovick, cloth, $10.00. Jasmine, Michael, and Noah are all regular kids except for one thing: Jasmine and Michael have two gay fathers. Noah has a gay mother. They have some unique concerns that they've never seen discussed by anyone else. This book, written by two lesbian mothers with help from their sons, will be a lifeline for other young people who face the same issues. It will also help their classmates, teachers, and parents to better understand just how varied today's families can be. Ages 6 to 12.
• "This title, with its multicultural cast of characters, its fresh line illustrations, and its emphasis on compassion rather than persuasion, is the sort of title that should be in the library of any child with gay or lesbian parents."
— *Bloomsbury Review*

ADULT BOOKS FROM ALYSON PUBLICATIONS

THE ALYSON ALMANAC, by Alyson Publications, $9.00. How did your representatives in Congress vote on gay issues? What are the best gay and lesbian books, movies, and plays? When was the first gay and lesbian march on Washington? With what king did Julius Caesar have a sexual relationship? You'll find all this, and more, in this unique and entertaining reference work.

BETWEEN FRIENDS, by Gillian E. Hanscombe, $8.00. The four women in this book represent radically different political outlooks and sexualities, yet they are tied together by the bonds of friendship. Through their experiences, recorded in a series of letters, Hanscombe deftly portrays the close relationship between political beliefs and everyday lives.

LESBIAN LISTS, by Dell Richards, $9.00. Lesbian holy days is just one of the hundreds of lists of clever and enlightening lesbian trivia compiled by columnist Dell Richards. Fun facts like uppity women who were called lesbians (but probably weren't), banned lesbian books, lesbians who've passed as men, herbal aphrodisiacs, black lesbian entertainers, and switch-hitters are sure to amuse and make *Lesbian Lists* a great gift.

CHOICES, by Nancy Toder, $9.00. Lesbian love can bring joy and passion; it can also bring conflicts. In this straightforward, sensitive novel, Nancy Toder conveys the fear and confusion of a woman coming to terms with her sexual and emotional attraction to other women.

UNBROKEN TIES, by Carol S. Becker, $10.00. Through a series of nearly one hundred personal accounts and interviews, Dr. Carol Becker, a practicing psychotherapist, charts the various stages of lesbian breakups and examines the ways in which women maintain ties with their former lovers. Becker shows how the end of a relationship can be a time of personal growth and how former lovers can form the core of an alternative family network.

THE WANDERGROUND, by Sally Miller Gearhart, $9.00. These absorbing, imaginative stories tell of a future women's culture, created in harmony with the natural world. The women depicted combine the control of mind and matter with a sensuous adherence to their own realities and history.

A MISTRESS MODERATELY FAIR, by Katherine Sturtevant, $9.00. Restoration England provides the setting for this vivid story of two women — one a playwright, the other an actress — who fall in love. Margaret Featherstone and Amy Dudley romp through a London peopled by nameless thousands and the titled few in a historical romance that is the most entertaining and best researched you'll ever read.

LONG TIME PASSING, edited by Marcy Adelman, $8.00. Here, in their own words, women talk about age-related concerns: the fear of losing a lover; the experience of being a lesbian in the 1940s and '50s; the issues of loneliness and community. Most contributors are older lesbians, but several younger voices are represented.

THE FIRST GAY POPE, by Lynne Yamaguchi Fletcher, $8.00. Everyone from trivia buffs to news reporters will enjoy this new reference book, which records hundreds of achievements, records, and firsts for the lesbian and gay community. What was the first lesbian novel by a woman? Where was the first gay civil rights law passed? When was the biggest gay demonstration? For the first time, the answers are all in one entertaining, well-indexed volume.

JOURNEY TO ZELINDAR, by Diana Rivers, $10.00. Sair grows up as the pampered daughter of an upper-caste family in a patriarchal city-state, but her life is forever changed by a brutal gang rape. Abandoned and left for dead, she makes her way to the ocean to kill herself. There she is rescued by the Hadra, wild riding-women who accept her into their culture. *Journey to Zelindar* is Sair's own tale of her adventures among the Hadra, who ride their horses by consent, speak mind-to-mind with each other, and are all lovers of women.

DAUGHTERS OF THE GREAT STAR, by Diana Rivers, $10.00. The daughters — the women who were born during the passing of the Great Star — possessed strange powers, which often they themselves did not understand. As they came of age, they found themselves estranged from their villages and even from their families. But as they were driven out of their childhood homes, they found one another, and created a community where they belonged. In this panoramic and exciting prequel to *Journey to Zelindar*, Diana Rivers portrays a world of strong and sensual women, ready to defend themselves against a hostile world without surrendering their ability to love each other.

WHAT I LOVE ABOUT LESBIAN POLITICS IS ARGUING WITH PEOPLE I AGREE WITH, by Kris Kovick, $8.00. The truth is funnier than fiction. Here's an inside look at the wry and occasionally warped mind of Kris Kovick, featuring some 140 of her cartoons, plus essays on religion and therapy ("I try to keep them separate, but it's hard"), lesbians and gay men, politics, sexuality, parenting, and American culture.

SUPPORT YOUR LOCAL BOOKSTORE

Most of the books described above are available at your nearest gay or feminist bookstore, and many of them will be available at other bookstores. If you can't get these books locally, order by mail using this form.

Enclosed is $_____ for the following books. (Add $1.00 postage when ordering just one book. If you order two or more, we'll pay the postage.)

1. _____

2. _____

3. _____

name: _____

address: _____

city: _____ state: _____ zip: _____

ALYSON PUBLICATIONS
Dept. H-80, 40 Plympton St., Boston, MA 02118

After June 30, 1994, please write for current catalog.